Olivia Says Goodbye to Grandpa

By Sarah, Duchess of York

Illustrated by Ian Cunliffe

STERLING

New York / London

STERLING and the distinctive Sterling logo are registered trademarks of
Sterling Publishing Co., Inc.

Library of Congress Cataloging-in-Publication Data Available

Lot #:
2 4 6 8 10 9 7 5 3 1
10/10
Published by Sterling Publishing Co., Inc.
387 Park Avenue South, New York, NY 10016
Story and illustrations © 2007 by Startworks Ltd.
"Ten Helpful Hints" © 2009 by Startworks Ltd.
Distributed in Canada by Sterling Publishing
c/o Canadian Manda Group, 165 Dufferin Street
Toronto, Ontario, Canada M6K 3H6
Distributed in Australia by Capricorn Link (Australia) Pty. Ltd.
P.O. Box 704, Windsor, NSW 2756, Australia

Printed in China
All rights reserved.

Sterling ISBN 978-1-4027-7394-5

For information about custom editions, special sales, premium and
corporate purchases, please contact Sterling Special Sales
Department at 800-805-5489 or specialsales@sterlingpublishing.com.

All children face many new experiences as they grow up, and helping them to understand and deal with each is one of the most demanding and rewarding things we do as parents. Helping Hand Books are for both children and parents to read, perhaps together. Each simple story describes a childhood experience and shows some of the ways in which to make it a positive one. I do hope these books encourage children and parents to talk about these sometimes difficult issues. Talking together goes a long way to finding a solution.

Sarah

Sarah, Duchess of York

Olivia loved her grandpa very much.

He had gray hair and a beard and was always smiling and laughing. Olivia liked it best when he told her stories and silly jokes. Grandpa laughed so loudly at his own jokes that Olivia just had to laugh, too.

Recently, Olivia's grandpa had not been well and he had to go to the hospital.

Olivia and her mom went to visit him. On the way, her mom said, "Grandpa may need us to cheer him up. Can you help me do that, Olivia?"

Olivia was sad to see her grandpa in the hospital. He looked weak and smaller than he did before. But she told him one of his silly jokes and tried to make him smile.

Olivia told her grandpa some of the fun things she had been doing at school.

"We took a trip to a farm last week, Grandpa," said Olivia. "There were huge cows and sheep with curly, woolly coats! You should have seen it, Grandpa!"

"There were goats, too. We were allowed to pet them. And they had beards just like yours!" she laughed. "I'll draw you a picture of a goat! Would you like that, Grandpa?"

"I would like that," said her grandpa. Then he smiled one of his warm smiles that Olivia loved so much.

A few mornings later, Olivia's mom and dad came into her bedroom. Olivia could see that her mom had been crying. Her dad sat on her bed and took her hand.

"I am afraid we have some very sad news," he said. "Grandpa passed away in his sleep last night."

At first, Olivia didn't really understand what her dad was saying.

"But I've almost finished the goat picture. I want him to see it," she cried.

"Grandpa would have loved your picture," said her mom gently. "I know he would want you to finish drawing it anyway."

Olivia's mom and dad hugged her tightly.

Over the next few days Olivia kept thinking about her grandpa. She imagined that he would soon be back, laughing and joking in his favorite chair. It was too hard to think that she would never see him again. Also, Olivia saw how sad her mom was. That made her sadder.

Olivia's parents knew she was sad about Grandpa, too. They let her stay home from school for a couple of days.

One night, Olivia was catching up on homework when her dad came to see her.

"How are you doing, sweethcart?" he asked.

Olivia just burst into tears.

"I'm so sad," she sobbed. "I don't think I will ever be happy again."

"Grandpa loved you very much," her dad said. "He would understand your sadness, but he would want you to remember all the times you laughed together, too."

"But what if someone else I love dies?" asked Olivia tearfully.

"I can understand your fear," said her dad. "But our time and energy need to go toward living our lives to the fullest. We must treat each day as special. Your grandpa certainly did that."

The next day, Olivia went back to school. Her friends knew she was sad and did their best to cheer her up. James, her best friend, gave her a hug, which really wasn't like him at all!

Olivia was happy that she had decided to go back to school instead of staying home and being sad.

In the classroom, Mrs. Collins settled everyone down.

"Olivia and I spoke before class today, and we both decided that a special way to honor her grandpa would be to have all of us write stories from our memories. Why don't we spend a few minutes thinking about someone special to each of us? Choose something memorable about that person to write a story about."

The students spent several minutes working on their stories.

When they were finished, Mrs. Collins asked for volunteers to read their stories to the class.

"Would any of you like to share your memory?" Mrs. Collins asked.

Some of the children's memories were so funny they made Olivia laugh out loud.

Jenny's aunt never took off her silly green hat. James's grandpa once tried to "cook" and burned the dinner. And Samantha's uncle wrote postcards from all over the world, forgot to mail them—and ended up bringing them home in his suitcase!

Olivia knew she had her own special memories to write about.

When Olivia got home from school, she saw that her mom had covered the table with photographs of her grandpa.

After dinner, Olivia and her mom and dad shared stories about Grandpa. They talked about the happy times they all had together.

That night, as Olivia lay in bed, she kept thinking about the story of her grandpa that she wrote for class. He had been so special and she knew she would miss him a lot.

"I will finish drawing that goat picture tomorrow," Olivia thought. "Grandpa would like that. He may not be here any longer, but I will remember him every time I look at that picture. Grandpa will always be in my happy memories."

TEN HELPFUL HINTS

TO HELP CHILDREN COPE WITH BEREAVEMENT

By Dr. Richard Woolfson, PhD

1. Encourage your child to use words to express what he is thinking and feeling about the bereavement. Let him know that it is perfectly all right to show emotions.

2. Try to be calm. When discussing bereavement with your child, remember that you are grieving, too. If you become distressed during the discussion, she is likely to become confused and afraid.

3. Listen carefully. Your child's feelings about grief are very real, and they can be intense. Children feel emotional pain just as adults do. Be there for your child as you would want someone to be there for you.

4. Give support. A warm hug from you may just be what he needs to help him through this difficult time. A loving gesture can ease his distress and can be more powerful than a long, serious discussion.

5. Make opportunities for creative play. Some children are able to work through their feelings with creative or imaginative play, perhaps by drawing or making something.

6. Your child might like to talk about the person who has died and bring out photographs and other reminders. Though this might be painful for you, it can be a useful part of the healing process, even when it takes place close to the bereavement.

7. Give lots of reassurance. The death of a friend or relative can make a child frightened and insecure. She may start to worry that others may die, too. She will need reassurance that everybody close to her is safe and well.

8. Give your child time. His pace of recovery from the loss of a loved one may take much longer than you would expect. Allow him time to adjust to the world without that person, however long that takes.

9. Explain death using your own words, whether religious or secular. It will feel more natural to you and will be the best way to explain it to your child.

10. Keep a close watch on your child in the days and weeks following the death. Look for any changes in her behavior that might indicate stress or depression. A shift in appetite, sleeping habits, and socialization might indicate a deepening problem.

Dr. Richard Woolfson is a child psychologist, working with children and their families. He is also an author and has written several books on child development and family life, in addition to numerous articles for magazines and newspapers. Dr. Woolfson runs training workshops for parents and child care professionals and appears regularly on radio and television. He is a Fellow of the British Psychological Society.

Helping Hand Books

Look for these other helpful books to share with your child: